W9-AQT-459

OHIO DOMINICAN UNIVERSITY
LIBRARY
1216 SUNBURY ROAD
COLUMBUS OHIO 43219-2099

J 782.42 Rog
Rogers, Sally.
Earthsong

EARTHSONG

Based on the popular song
"Over in the Endangered Meadow"

by SALLY ROGERS

illustrated by MELISSA BAY MATHIS

JUN 2005
Received
Ohio Dominican

DUTTON CHILDREN'S BOOKS · NEW YORK

Text copyright © 1998 by Sally Rogers
Illustrations copyright © 1998 by Melissa Bay Mathis
Based on the song "Over in the Endangered Meadow," by Sally Rogers;
from a traditional melody; arrangement copyright © 1997 by Sally Rogers.
Inspired by the poem "Over in the Meadow," by Olive Wadsworth
All rights reserved.

CIP Data is available.

Published in the United States 1998 by Dutton Children's Books,
a member of Penguin Putnam Inc.
375 Hudson Street, New York, New York 10014
Designed by Amy Berniker
Printed in Hong Kong   First Edition
10 9 8 7 6 5 4 3 2 1
ISBN 0-525-45673-5

Acknowledgments: The Pittsburgh Aviary,
The Cincinnati Zoo (Thane Maynard and Stan Rullman),
Kristen Karpf, Chuck Tague, and Sandra Willoughby

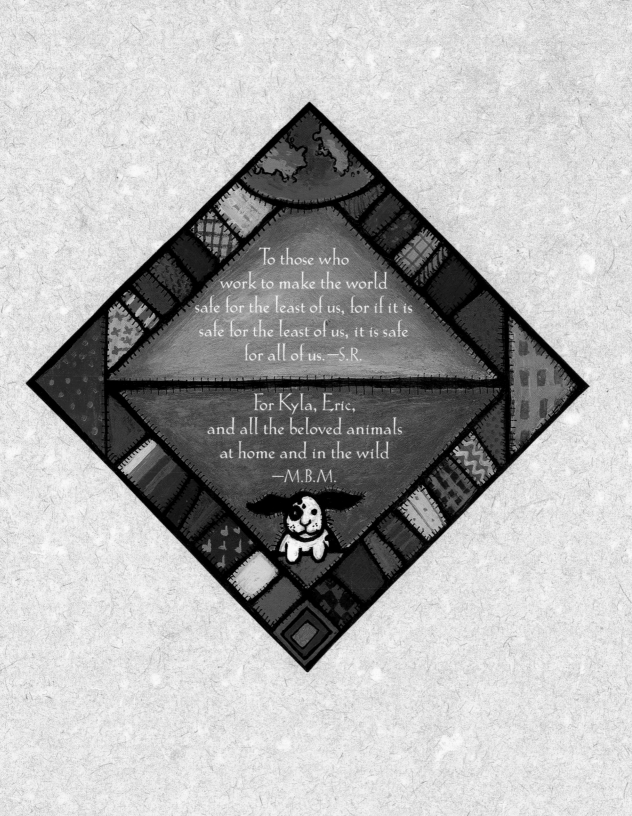

To those who
work to make the world
safe for the least of us, for if it is
safe for the least of us, it is safe
for all of us. —S.R.

For Kyla, Eric,
and all the beloved animals
at home and in the wild
—M.B.M.

In my grandparents' parlor was an overstuffed chair.
We climbed up in my grandpa's lap when he sat there.
"Sing!" said my grandpa. "Let's sing!" said we.
And this is what we sang upon my grandpa's knee:

In the North Atlantic Ocean 'neath the Arctic sun
Lived a mom and papa right whale and their whale calf one.
"Blow!" said the mother. "I blow!" said the one.
And they blew and they spouted 'neath the Arctic sun.

Far away in China where the bamboo grew
Lived a young mother panda and her little pandas two.
"Chew!" said the mother. "We chew!" said the two.
And they chewed in far-off China where the bamboo grew.

In the Bangladeshi jungles where the tigers roam free
Lived a mother Bengal tiger and her little cubs three.
"Pounce!" said the mother. "We pounce!" said the three.
And they pounced in the jungles where the tigers roam free.

In the Gujarati forest where the serpent eagles soar,
An Asiatic lioness groomed her golden cubs four.
"Roar!" said the mother. "We roar!" squeaked the four.
And they roared in the forest where the serpent eagles soar.

At the mouth of a tunnel where the prairie dogs dive
Stood a black-footed ferret and her little ferrets five.
"Stand still!" said the mother. "We will," said the five.
And they stood at attention where the prairie dogs dive.

'Neath the rain-forest canopy where monkeys play their tricks
Flew a sun conure mother and her noisy nestlings six.
"Shriek!" said the mother. "We shriek!" squawked the six.
And they shrieked through the canopy as monkeys played their tricks.

In the Arizona desert in the heat of one-eleven
Lived a mother Gila monster and her little monsters seven.
"Strike!" said the mother. "We strike!" said the seven.
And they stuck their little tongues out in the heat of one-eleven.

On a beach their mother visited again and again,
The leatherback turtles hatched, eight, nine, ten...
"Swim!" said some others. "We swim!" said the ten.
And they swam from the beach, but they'll come back again.

On the frigid Arctic tundra where auroras paint the heavens
Lived a grizzled momma gray wolf and her pack of pups eleven.
"Howl!" growled the mother. "We howl!" growled the eleven.
And they howled on the tundra where auroras paint the heavens.

In the swampy Florida keys south of Lake Okeechobee,
A mother croc taught her babies, twenty, thirty, forty.
"Paddle!" urged the mother. "We paddle!" pipped the forty.
And they paddled in the swamps south of Lake Okeechobee.

Coiled round her nest of eggs for fifty lonely days,
A mother python longed to watch her hundred snakelets play.
"Hatch!" said the mother. "We'll hatch!" they hummed for days.
And finally, when they hatched, she watched her snakelets play.

Fin, fur, and feather and the human race
Must share Mother Earth as she spins through space.
"Share!" says my grandpa. "Please share this place!
And we'll care for Mother Earth as she spins through space."

Notes on the Animals

NORTH ATLANTIC RIGHT WHALE ✣ These are among the most endangered whales. Approximately 150 individuals are known to overwinter in Cape Cod Bay, and only a few hundred are estimated to swim in the Atlantic waters. Right whales were hunted to near extinction by commercial whalers, who considered them to be the "right" whale to hunt—because they are slower than other baleen whales and float after they have been killed. An international ban on whaling may allow these giants to make a comeback.

PANDA ✣ Pandas live in China, where they eat quantities of bamboo. Unfortunately, bamboo is becoming harder and harder to find as the human population encroaches on the pandas' territory. As a result, the number of pandas has dwindled to fewer than one thousand in the wild. Several zoos are attempting to breed pandas, but these efforts are not enough to offset the panda population that has been lost.

BENGAL TIGER ✣ This elegant, swift creature raises its young among the mangrove trees in the Sundarbans jungle of Bangladesh, formerly East Bengal. The tigers are so fierce that the locals will not hunt them for fear of being ambushed by the animals. Bengal tigers rear an average litter of two or three—five is the maximum. Tiger kits learn to hunt from their mother. Destruction of their mangrove habitat, as well as hunting, have endangered them.

ASIATIC, OR INDIAN, LION ✣ These lions are similar in size to their African cousins but have smaller manes. When India was a British colony, sportsmen hunted the Asiatic lion to near extinction. The lions' range is now limited to the dry grasslands of the Gir Forest in India's western state of Gujarat. Three to five cubs is the average litter. Although protected by the government, the lions' safe haven is threatened by India's growing population.

BLACK-FOOTED FERRET ✣ The black-footed ferret is a relative of the ferrets that are kept as house pets. But its fate is nowhere near as secure. Black-footed ferrets eat prairie dogs, so mothers teach their babies to lie in wait at the mouths of prairie dog burrows. When prairie dogs stick their noses out in the open, the ferrets pounce on them for a fine feast.

Farmers in the midwestern United States often poison prairie dogs to keep them from eating crops. Although there are still plenty of prairie dogs (they reproduce frequently, with large litters), ferrets have fallen victim both to the poison and to a lack of food. Ferrets do not reproduce very rapidly, so they have been added to the endangered list.

SUN CONURE ✣ This noisy, bright yellow bird lives in the forest regions of northern South America (southeastern Venezuela, Guyana, French Guiana, and northeastern Brazil), where it makes a nest of sticks in the holes of dead trees. Although females have been known to lay six eggs, three to four eggs is their normal clutch. As the rain forest is cut down, so is the habitat of the sun conure.

GILA MONSTER ✣ The Gila monster is not a monster at all, but a lizard that lives in the deserts of the southwestern United States. Though it grows to a length of two feet, a Gila monster is only six inches long when it hatches. The Gila monster has an interesting tail. The tails of many lizards break off in the mouths of their enemies when they need to escape; but the fat, stubby tail of the Gila monster doesn't break off. Instead, it stores fat for times when food is scarce. Gila monsters spend most of the day sheltered in burrows, coming out at night to eat insects and small animals. They lunge quickly at their prey and kill it with venom from their jaws. The Gila monster's habitat has been threatened by agricultural activity and cattle grazing.

LEATHER-BACK TURTLE ✣ This beautiful sea turtle suffers on many fronts, threatened by ocean pollution and the hunting of its eggs. When it's time, a mother leatherback turtle returns to the sandy beach where she herself once hatched. There she deposits her eggs, then heads back to the sea. After fifty-three to seventy-four days, the baby turtles hatch. The line in the text says the turtles hatch "eight, nine, ten…"

but mother leatherbacks lay eighty to one hundred eggs. When the young females are mature and ready to lay their eggs, they in turn come back to the spot where they hatched—if they survive their dangerous lives.

GRAY WOLF ✦ Although a mother gray wolf bears only five or six pups at a time, they are cared for in packs that include adults and pups from other wolf famlies. Hence the count of eleven in the text. Because of fairy tales and stories of werewolves and the like, wolves have been feared by humans for centuries. Farmers and ranchers worry that they will kill livestock, so many gray wolves have been poisoned or shot. Some states even offer bounties on wolf pelts. Despite opposition, attempts are being made to reintroduce these endangered animals into national forests.

AMERICAN CROCODILE ✦ The American alligator has been removed from the list of endangered species, but its cousin, the American crocodile, continues to hover at the brink of extinction. It lives only in isolated hamlets of brackish water in the southernmost part of Florida and the Keys. Encroachment by human populations has been the biggest reason for its loss of habitat.

A mother croc makes a nest mound of soil, then digs a hole in it where she lays her twenty to forty eggs. She stays near her nest for a period of seventy to eighty days, and when she hears her babies calling from inside the eggs, she knows it's time for them to hatch. She scrapes away the soil to uncover them and then carries them in her mouth to water close by. Instinct tells the babies to swim. Still, they often stay close to their mother for several months before heading off on their own.

INDIAN PYTHON ✦ Reaching a length of twenty feet, the Indian python is considered to be only medium size in the python world. The largest clutch of eggs on record is 107. Because the nest is shallow and at ground level, and because the mother fasts while coiled on top of her eggs for the two months it takes them to hatch, mother and eggs are vulnerable to both human and animal predators. Humans collect these pythons for the world pet trade and for their skins. Agriculture has also destroyed some of their habitat.